GROSSET & DUNLAP
An imprint of Penguin Random House LLC, New York

First published in the United States of America by Grosset & Dunlap,
an imprint of Penguin Random House LLC, New York, 2022

GROSSET & DUNLAP is a registered trademark of Penguin Random House LLC.

Visit us online at penguinrandomhouse.com.

Library of Congress Cataloging-in-Publication Data is available.

Manufactured in China

ISBN 9780593521748   10 9 8 7 6 5 4 3 2 1 HH

Design by Sophie Erb

An **Anna Dewdney** Book

love from
llama
llama

Grosset & Dunlap

Love is . . .

Sunny mornings
spent with Mama . . .

Hugs from Grandpa,

a kiss from Grandma.

Love is with your
friends outside . . .

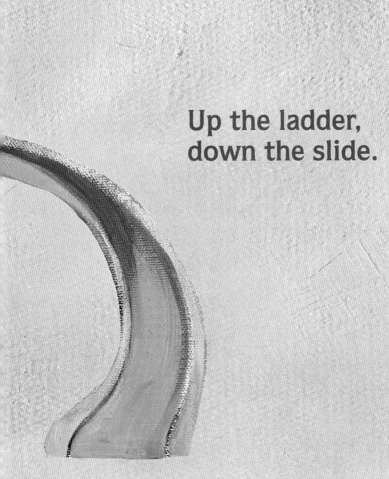

Up the ladder,
down the slide.

Love is for your
teachers, too . . .

Those who guide and those who soothe.

Love is for your
Fuzzy friend . . .

Whose love for
you has no end.

And even when you
pout and shout . . .

Love will be there,
have no doubt.

And when the sun
sets down so low . . .

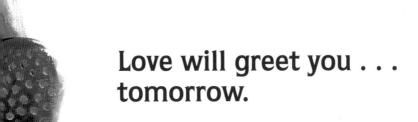

Love will greet you . . .
tomorrow.